PUFFIN BOOKS

HAIRY AND SLUG

Hairy is a large, very shaggy brown dog. Slug is an ancient, obstinate little white car. Both belong to the Mablesden family, a perfectly ordinary family leading perfectly ordinary lives. But it's surprising how often a perfectly ordinary day turns out to be rather exciting, especially when Hairy and Slug are around. A trip out to the country, an outing to the seaside, a visit to the carnival – all these seem to involve Hairy and Slug in the most amazing adventures! They catch a thief, get stopped by the police and even win a prize at the County Show!

These friendly and amusing stories will be much loved by young readers.

Margaret Joy was born on Tyneside. After living for some years on Teeside, where she taught in a sixth-form college and later became a full-time teacher of five-year-olds, she moved to North Wales where her husband is head of a school for deaf children. They have four children. Margaret Joy has written several stories for young children, some of which have been featured on *Play School* and *Listen with Mother*. Her *Tales from Allotment Lane School* is published in Young Puffin.

Hairy and Slug

MARGARET JOY

Illustrated by Rowena Allen

PUFFIN BOOKS
in association with
Faber and Faber

PUFFIN BOOKS

Published by the Penguin Group
27 Wrights Lane, London W8 5TZ, England
Viking Penguin Inc., 40 West 23rd Street, New York, New York 10010, USA
Penguin Books Australia Ltd, Ringwood, Victoria, Australia
Penguin Books Canada Ltd, 2801 John Street, Markham, Ontario, Canada L3R 1B4
Penguin Books (NZ) Ltd, 182–190 Wairau Road, Auckland 10, New Zealand

Penguin Books Ltd, Registered Offices: Harmondsworth, Middlesex, England

First published by Faber and Faber Limited 1983
Published in Puffin Books 1985
Reprinted 1986 (twice), 1987 (twice), 1988

Made and printed in Great Britain by
Richard Clay Ltd, Bungay, Suffolk

Contents

I

SLUG AND THE POLICE CAR

·——◆——·

There was once a car called the Little White Slug. If it opened its doors very wide and breathed in deeply, four people could *just* squeeze in—two at the front and two at the back. And a big hairy, brown dog could *just* crawl in and lie squashed very uncomfortably on the floor below the back seat.

Even then, the four people had to lean towards each other and keep their elbows tucked well in before they slammed the doors. Then the Little White Slug would bounce on its springs as the doors slammed, the tyres would flatten a little, the glass in the window frames would judder, and the seats would make groaning, wheezing noises as the air was pressed out of them.

Bang! Wham! Slam! Bang! went the four doors.

Doi-oi-oi-oing! went the springs.

Rak-a-tak-a-rak-a-tak! went the window glass.

Eeesh, sheesh, eeesh, wheeeee! wheezed the seats.

Akakakakakaka-a! gasped the Little White Slug, as Tom, the driver, tried the ignition. But the engine died away immediately.

"Come on, Slug," cried Tom, pushing his glasses up on his nose. "We've got to get to the petrol station before it closes. Come on, you've got hardly any petrol left in your tank!"

"Brrmmm, brrrmmm," grumbled the Little White Slug, starting up very slowly. "You've let my petrol get down really low. It would serve you right if I hadn't enough to get to the petrol station."

Very slowly she rumbled down the road, looking for every pot-hole to lurch into and swerving over drain covers in the gutter—on purpose! She'd give them a ride to remember. They'd been neglecting her—fancy letting her petrol get down so low.

"Come on, Slug," yelled Brian and Maria in the back.

"Rruff! Yes, come on, you old tin can," barked Hairy, the dog. "Let's get this over and done with, so I can get back to the telly." Hairy was a telly-fiend; he was always at his happiest sitting in front of the television.

"Yes, come on, Slug," urged Annie, who was sitting in the front next to her husband, Tom. She patted the dashboard encouragingly. "Come on, Slug, we're nearly there."

But the Little White Slug was sulky. She'd had nothing to drink for days, and now they were expecting her to rush along like a white tornado. Well, she wasn't called Slug for nothing—she'd show them! She started to slow down: thirty miles an hour, twenty-five, twenty, fifteen . . . her engine began to jerk and splutter.

"Look, there's the petrol station at the end of the road," said Annie. "Nearly there, Slug." But the Little White Slug was crawling along at five miles an hour in a very sulky mood. Then she stopped.

Tom got out and slammed the door. "Bother you, Slug!" he said, smacking her smartly on the bonnet. He began to push the car the rest of the way to the petrol pumps. They got there at last and Brian and Maria cheered loudly.

"Hello," said bald Mr Fortescue, the petrol pump attendant. He was an old friend. "Being a bit sluggish, is she?" Laughing at his own joke, he unscrewed Slug's petrol cap and pushed the nozzle of the pump into the hole.

Whooosh-sh-sh! The petrol poured into Slug's insides. "Mmmm. *That's* better," she thought. "What a marvellous smell! Now I feel better. I'm full up again at last—they left me *gasping* for petrol for days."

Mr Fortescue shook the last drops off the nozzle and screwed the petrol cap on again. Tom paid him and got in. The Little White Slug started immediately. "Brrrmmm," she shouted happily. "Hurray! My goodness, I needed that. Off we go then." The speedometer needle started to move round: thirty miles an hour, thirty-five, forty, forty-five, fifty, fifty-five . . . !

"Hold on," shouted Tom to Slug.

"I *am*!" shouted Annie, clutching the sides of her seat. They had to shout to be heard above the rattling, wheezing noises Slug was making as she raced along. "I don't think this speed is very good for Slug; she's not used to it."

"It's lovely, lovely, faster, faster," cried Maria and Brian in the back. They were being bounced up and down like ping-pong balls. Hairy was lying flat on the floor at their feet, howling softly to himself. He didn't like being in the white tin can at any time, and especially not when there was one of his favourite programmes on telly.

"We're doing fifty-five," shrieked Brian, looking over his father's shoulder.

Tom was finding it difficult to keep his hands steady on the vibrating steering wheel, as Slug was bombing along at fifty-five—something she'd never been known to do before. She bounced over pebbles and bumps in the road,

her headlights gleaming in the sunshine and an excited grin over her radiator grille.

Suddenly: Dah-der, dah-der, dah-der . . . ! Brian and Maria scrambled up on their seat and looked back. A sleek white car with POLICE written across it was zooming up behind and overtaking. The round blue light on its roof was flashing menacingly. The police car shot ahead of the Little White Slug and an illuminated message flashed at them: STOP.

Tom put on the brakes and Slug squealed and panted to a halt. One of the two policemen in the car got out and slowly walked round to where Slug was snorting and steaming after her wild race along the road. "This is a thirty miles an hour stretch," said the policeman, folding his arms and looking down at Tom. Tom swallowed and blinked up at him.

"I couldn't help it, really, Officer. It was the car—it was Slug, she just started to race away. I couldn't do a thing with her."

"You expect me to believe that?" chortled the policeman. "It was the *car's* fault? Hey, Jeff, come and listen to this." The second policeman got out and walked slowly back to the little white car.

Slug had been looking carefully at the police car's number plate. "Hey!" she said. "It's COP 999Z. I know you. Didn't we meet in that underground car park last summer? Do you remember? And you said my hub caps needed seeing to?"

"Oh, it's you, is it?" grunted the police car. "Yes, I remember you perfectly. You said there was nothing wrong with your hub caps, and then as soon as you drove away, one of them fell off and rolled along the length of the car park. Someone had to run after you and get your driver to stop and put your hub cap on for you. It gave me a good laugh, that did."

"I'm glad of that," said Slug, swallowing her pride, "but I tell you what—can you get me out of trouble again? It looks as though your two chaps are getting stroppy with my lot."

Slug was right. Tom was sitting meekly in his seat, while the two tall policemen stood in their shirt sleeves, looking down suspiciously at Slug and her passengers. "I'm sorry, sir," said the first policeman. "Your car could not have carried you along at fifty, if you hadn't wanted it to. No car can do things by itself."

"No, no car at all," nodded Jeff in agreement.

"Come on, come on," muttered Slug out of the corner of her radiator grille. "*Do* something, COP 999Z!" Suddenly the police car's back nearside indicator started to flash bright orange – BLINK – pause – BLINK – pause – BLINK . . .

"Hey, look at that!" said Tom. He and Annie craned their necks out of their windows to see.

BLINK – pause – BLINK – pause – BLINK!

"It's doing it all by itself," shouted Brian.

"All by itself," echoed Maria. They both craned their necks out of *their* windows. Jeff and his friend were standing open-mouthed, and they were blinking too. Then the police car's two red brake lights came on.

"I thought no car could do things by itself . . ." murmured Tom. The two policemen seemed unable to move. Then the blue light on top of their car started to flash.

"How'm I doing?" murmured the police car to Slug.

"Fantastic!" Slug hissed back. "How about the siren too?"

"OK," said the police car obligingly. "Dah-der, dah-der, dah-der," he wailed at full volume. That did it. The two policemen raced to their car, scrambled in as fast as they could and slammed the doors. The lights went out. The siren stopped.

The driver put out a hand and impatiently waved Slug to drive on past them. Very slowly and carefully Tom steered Slug out past the police car and along the road again. As she went past him, Slug winked her offside indicator at COP 999Z in gratitude. "It's sometimes useful to have friends in high places," she thought smugly to herself, and settled down to her usual steady crawl of twenty-five miles per hour.

"Perhaps now at last we can get home to 'Coronation Street'," growled Hairy.

2
SLUG AND THE
CAR WASH

———◆———

It was Sunday afternoon. "Time for walkies, Hairy!"
said Maria, taking the dog's lead off the hook on the
wall. Hairy was watching the television and took no
notice. He thumped his tail excitedly as the sheriff and
his men had a shoot-out with the bandits in a rocky
canyon.

"Come on, Hairy, it's time for walkies," said Maria
again.

"Switch it off, for goodness sake, or he'll sit glued to it
all day," said Annie in exasperation. "You'll get to be a
fat, unhealthy dog, Hairy."

"Your fur will be dull and lifeless," said Tom.

"You'll get rolls of fat round your middle, like the
Michelin tyre man," said Brian.

"You won't be able to run—only waddle," said Maria.

Hairy howled dismally, but no one knew if it was
because of what they were saying or because the sheriff
and the bandits had been switched off.

"Tell you what," said Tom, "we'll go for a spin in the
country—"

"A *spin*?"

"In Slug?"

"A crawl, you mean."

"All right then—let's go for a crawl in the country.

Then Hairy can get plenty of exercise and we can get a breath of fresh air. Come on: everybody out!"

The Little White Slug saw them all walking briskly down the path towards her, pulling an unwilling dog behind them. She knew what that meant: a drive into the muddy countryside. As they opened the four doors, she breathed in. Slam! Slam! Slam! At last they bundled in the unwilling hairy creature, and—Slam! Slug relaxed again.

Tom guided her through lanes which were thick with fallen leaves and dirt dropped from farm tractor tyres. Slug had to slosh through huge puddles and along muddy rutted tracks. Annie opened her front window right down.

"Mmm," she said. "Isn't the air fresh?" She breathed in deeply. "I *love* being out in the country, don't you?"

"No," snarled Hairy to himself. "I'll never know who shot the sheriff now."

"No," muttered Slug. "It's filthy. I get dirt in my tyre treads, insects on my windscreen, mud splashes on my paintwork—fancy making any self-respecting car *white*, I ask you. And it's even worse when they all come charging back in again."

Slug was right. The family stopped her on a cart-track just inside a wood and rushed off to play hide and seek behind the trees. Even Hairy stopped sulking and leapt about in the bracken and moss, barking at beetles and bouncing over brambles. A gusty wind was blowing and pine needles started to ping down on to Slug's roof.

"I've had enough of Nature," announced Brian at last, panting for breath.

"Yes, I think I have too," agreed Maria. They all made their way back to the Little White Slug.

Annie opened the boot and pushed in several long

branches of copper beech leaves. Tom heaved in a huge log he had found. "Thought it would make a nice bird-table base," he said. "Sort of rustic."

Slug groaned. She hated nasty tickly leaves in her boot, especially when creepy-crawlies might emerge and scuttle round inside her. And then came the moment she dreaded: two back doors were wrenched open and Maria and Brian leapt in with a bounce that made Slug's springs squeak. Pine needles fell off their clothes and worked their way down between the seats. Lumps of mud fell off their shoes onto the floor.

Then Hairy came galloping back and scrabbled in, leaving dirty pawprints on Slug's silver trim and showering muddy drops from his fur all over the back seat and floor. Slug shuddered. "I shall be filthy inside and out," she thought. "They never consider *my* feelings. . ."

Tom got in, but Annie went round to the front of Slug with a bunch of heather she'd picked. "Oh, no, not that," thought Slug. "It looks so silly. All the big lorries laugh at me. Besides, it makes me sneeze!"

But Annie did what Slug feared: she pushed the stems of the heather into the radiator grille. "There," she said, standing back to admire the effect. "That's supposed to be lucky. Now you're a . . . a . . . Lucky Slug!" She hurried round to get in her door and didn't see Slug gnash her radiator grille bars at her.

When Tom turned on the ignition, Slug just snarled angrily, then stopped. Tom tried again, and Slug sneezed loudly twice, then stopped again. Tom looked worried and said, "Must have got her plugs damp."

"Soaked, you mean," snapped Slug and started to stutter jerkily, then moved off so suddenly that they all fell backwards in their seats. That made her feel better, so she took them towards home at nearly twenty-eight miles an hour. Then she realized that Tom was steering her towards Mr Fortescue's petrol station. "But I don't need any petrol today," she thought. "What's he bringing me here for?"

Tom steered Slug past the petrol pumps and down the side of the repair shop and round the back. Slug had never been here before. "Aha!" said Tom. "Thought I'd surprise you all. Old Fortescue's opened a Car Wash. We'll give Slug a shampoo and a blow dry—get rid of all that country muck."

He pulled Slug to a halt and opened his window to push some coins into a slot machine. "Ready, everyone?" he asked. "Shut your windows tight and—in we go!" He drove slowly into a large dark sort of shed. On the right a huge green bristly brush stretched from floor to ceiling; there was another on the left and a third hung from the roof. Tom switched off the engine. Silence. Suddenly there was a roaring sound.

Slug was terrified. She'd never been in a car wash before and didn't know what was going to happen. The roaring noise was growing louder, and the great green bristly brushes started to spin round at a dizzy speed. ("They must be doing about seventy," thought Slug, horrified.)

Then the roaring, whirling bristles started to move towards Slug. They rolled up and down her radiator grille, spitting tiny droplets of water all over her bonnet and her windscreen. Meanwhile the side brushes were scrubbing her mudguards and her doors and tyres, and then they were bristling over her roof and boot. Water was cascading all over her, making her shudder and shiver, and the brushes were tickling her terribly, poking and bristling, making her bounce up and down.

"Ouch, that tickles," she shrieked. "Don't do that—I've got sensitive hub-caps. You've no right to squirt water all over my lights!"

But the brushes were making such a noise with their rolling and spinning and squirting that no one heard her. The vibrating and shaking made Slug very cross indeed. "I'll soon stop them," she thought. And as the green brushes started to roll back again for another tickling session, all her windows very gently and slowly eased down a few centimetres.

None of her passengers noticed. They were too busy watching the growling green brushes. Even Hairy had managed to scramble up on the back seat between Maria and Brian; watching what was happening through the back window made it almost like television. Suddenly Maria screamed, "I'm getting wet!"

"I'm getting soaked," yelled Brian.

Jets of water poured through the side windows on to the children, soaking their clothes, their hair, their faces, everything. Streams of water poured over Hairy, and the back seat of the car was awash. Before Tom and Annie were fully aware of what was happening and why, the brushes were spinning past their own open windows: whoosh! Sprays of water poured over Tom's head, streamed down his spectacles, waterfalled on to his lap. Annie's hair was soaked and her perm started to frizz up into tiny curls. Water sprayed over the dashboard on to their knees, and puddled on the rubber matting at their feet. Then, unexpectedly, the roaring stopped and the brushes stood in front of them again, dripping quietly.

Inside the car there was pandemonium. Water was trickling everywhere. "I told you all to shut the

windows!" snapped Tom, wiping his glasses on his vest, the only dry material he could find.

"We did shut them, tight," said Maria, her teeth chattering. Hairy shook himself with all his might. Droplets of water flew to every corner of the car.

"Oh, HAIRY!" they all shouted.

"Come on," said Tom, "let's get Slug dried, then we can all drive home." He drove the car forward to the front of the shed. Gusts of warm air blew soothingly over Slug and dried up all the drops of water in the cracks and crevices. She had to admit that after the ordeal of the scrubbing brushes, this was very pleasant. The glass in her lights and windows was sparkling. Acorns and pine needles had been brushed off her roof, which was now gleaming white. All the mud splashes and filthy pawprints had disappeared. She was even clean behind her mudguards—always a place that tended to get neglected.

Tom drove them straight home to change their clothes. As they cruised past the High Street shops, Slug was able to see her gleaming white reflection moving trimly past the shop windows. She smiled complacently. Yes, she *was* a neat little car, no doubt about it.

As the family climbed out to rush into the house and change into dry things, Tom said, "We'll come out soon and dry you up too, Slug." Hairy galloped away up the front steps; it would soon be time for 'Songs of Praise', and he didn't mean to miss a note of it.

"Oh dear, look," said Annie, as she squeezed water from her wet curls. "That silly car wash has even washed out my pretty bunch of heather. And it was supposed to be lucky."

"It *was* lucky for me," thought Slug, flashing a bright chrome grin with her radiator grille. "Perhaps they'll think twice about getting me so dirty in future . . ."

3
SLUG AND SEASIDE SID

It was already warm and sunny at eight o'clock one morning. Annie was packing a huge picnic basket of cheese, tomato, ham and salad rolls, a couple of packets of biscuits, some crisps and apples, a bottle of lemonade, and a bottle of water for Hairy.

Maria and Brian had filled a bag with their swimming things and towels and were wiping the cobwebs off their buckets and spades, which had been in the shed since the previous year. Maria had her new Instamatic camera slung round her neck. Hairy was moping round the house, as he had realized that an Outing was being planned and that there would be no television all day. Still, at least he could make sure they got home in good time for evening viewing. He picked up the folded *Radio Times* between his teeth and trotted down the path to the car. There he sat, still holding the magazine and patiently waiting for the family to join him.

Tom already had his sunglasses on and was putting the cricket bat, a ball and a blanket into Slug's boot. He piled in all the rest of the things, then checked Slug's oil, water and tyre pressures. "Slug, old girl," he said, coaxingly wiping her windscreen with a soft yellow duster, "do you think you can manage a stretch of motorway today? We all fancy a trip to the sea, so I hope you'll make it. Don't be put off by those great lorries thundering past—just trust in me, and cruise along steadily. I think you'll enjoy a day out, Slug."

By half past eight they were on the motorway. The Little White Slug wasn't used to driving on such a wide, busy road, but she did as Tom told her and they chugged steadily along the inside lane. The monster lorries were rather frightening; they were so high and so long. They roared past so quickly that they seemed to leave a strong gust of wind behind them which rocked the little white car on her springs.

But there was a great deal to look at. "There's a kestrel," said Maria, pointing to a bird hovering with outstretched wings, almost without moving, above the grassy bank at the side of the motorway.

"Oh, look at the cows up there," said Brian.

"Cows up where?" asked his mother in a bewildered voice.

"Going over that bridge in front of us," answered Brian. "We'll be underneath them in a moment. And that'll be the sixteenth bridge we've been under."

After a while they played one of their number plate games. "GRG," called out Tom, reading from the car in front.

"Garage," said Maria.

"Gargling," said Annie.

"Um . . . George," said Brian.

"Not allowed," said Maria and her mother together. "No names!"

"All right, then," said Brian, peering at a car passing them in the middle lane. "How about XTR?"

"Extra," said Maria.

"Extremely," said Tom.

"Foxtrot," said Annie triumphantly.

"Wow, that's a cunning one," said Tom.

They stopped playing when Maria suddenly announced, "First to see the sea! First to see the sea!" They all looked eagerly to where a thin blue line met the different blue of the sky away beyond the rooftops of the seaside town. Slug turned slowly off the motorway and along the main street. The houses had that special look of seaside houses, painted pale blue, bright pink or cream, with swinging signboards or little notices in the front window, which read "Bed and Breakfast," or simply "B & B".

Tom managed to find an empty parking space on the sea front. While the family unloaded everything, Hairy sat sniffing the unfamiliar smells of seaweed, fish and candy floss. He had never seen so many legs pass by before, some in trousers, some in jeans, but mostly bare legs: hairy, tanned, pink, brown, long and slim, short and plump, and all with bare feet and five toes. Hairy sniffed at them eagerly.

"Come on, Hairy, let's find a bit of sand to ourselves," called Brian. Hairy galloped after him, and the others followed.

"Wait a minute," said Maria. "I want to take some photos."

"Wait till we get settled on the beach," said her mother. "Tom, have you got the picnic? And the blanket? And the chairs?" Poor Tom staggered down the steps after the others.

Slug thought, "You haven't locked me, Tom! Hey, come back and lock me." But Tom was struggling away across the beach, weighed down with luggage, his shoes already full of soft sand.

"Isn't it a relief when they get out?" asked a cheerful
voice on Slug's left. She looked round. A small blue car
was parked there.

Slug could see a baby seat strapped in the back. She
said, "Yes, it's quite a strain concentrating on the other
traffic when you've got a yelling toddler with you, isn't
it?" She still remembered hectic sticky journeys with
Brian and Maria squabbling and covering her upholstery
with chocolate, and then having to open all the windows
when they felt sick.

The blue car said, "Still, at least they've parked us
where we can see what's going on. I hate those multi-
storey places, don't you? Nothing to see except a concrete
wall, and then you're left in the dark anyway. They give
me the creeps."

"I quite agree," said Slug. "Now this is more like it. All
these people to look at, and the boats on the sea out there.
That's a big one, look, with smoke coming up out of its
exhaust. I wonder how many horse power it is . . ."

The blue car didn't answer. He was watching a crowd of
people standing admiring a large bronze-coloured car
nearby. It was a huge powerful machine, the latest model,
with the latest registration plate.

"Hey, look at him," said the blue car.

"Yes, very swish, isn't he?" agreed Slug.

"No, I don't mean the new car," the blue car answered.
"I mean *him*, that man there in the black blazer."

"He's looking at the new car," said Slug. "What's
wrong with that?"

"He's just pulled that other man's wallet out of his back
trouser pocket," said the blue car.

"Stolen his petrol money?" exclaimed Slug. "That's
awful! Let's watch him and see if he does it again."

They both watched the man in the black blazer. He was moving slowly round the crowd of men and boys who were admiring the streamlined bronze model. "Watch!" hissed the blue car. The man's hand was slyly reaching out to another back trouser pocket where a brown wallet was sticking out.

"He's got it," breathed Slug. They watched as the man slid the wallet into the inside pocket of his blazer. Then he strolled away from the crowd and stood near the two cars, pretending to look out over the beach. The men whose money had been stolen still hadn't realized that their wallets were gone.

The man in the black blazer now turned and strolled towards the line of cars parked on the sea front. He went up to a green saloon and quietly tried the door handle. Luckily the car was locked.

"He's coming nearer," whispered the blue car.

"And they've not locked me," Slug hissed back, horrified. "And Annie's left her purse in my glove compartment!"

The man was casually trying the door of the mustard-coloured estate car on the far side of the little blue one. It was locked. "Help, it's me next," said the blue car, and stood motionless with fright. Again, the man quietly pushed down the door handle, but it didn't move.

Slug had been thinking quickly. While the man was hidden from view at the other side of the blue car, she had let her side window slip down a few centimetres. Now she was standing alert on the balls of her tyres, tense and ready for instant action . . .

The man was slowly coming round the back of Slug, approaching the passenger's window. He glanced inside and immediately saw the red purse in the glove compartment. Casually looking round to make sure that he wasn't being watched, he slid his hand through the crack at the top of the window. Then he pushed down hard to open it further.

Slug was too quick for him. She slammed the window upward as hard as she possibly could. The man let out a piercing yell as his hand was caught by Slug's cruel upper-cut. He was quite unable to move, however hard he jerked and pulled to free himself. At the same time Slug was sounding her horn as hard as she ever had in her life: Baaarp! Baaarp!

"That sounds like Slug's horn," said Maria, as she took photos of the family on the beach. She ran back up to the sea front to find out.

"Baaarp! Baaarp! Baaarp!"

"That sounds like fun," said the little blue car. "I'll help you." And he started to sound *his* horn: "Beep-beeep! Beep-beeep!"

"Aaaagh!" yelled the man in the black blazer, still pulling desperately at his squeezed hand.

A police motor-cyclist who was patrolling the sea front heard the dreadful noise. He wheeled his motor bike sharply round and rode back to the disturbance. A crowd was gathering.

"Look, he's got his hand caught."

"Why doesn't he just unlock his door and open the window from the inside?"

"That's not his car," exclaimed Maria, who had just run up in her bathing costume, still holding the camera. "That's my Dad's car. What's he doing trying to get into my Dad's car?" She very sensibly stood still to focus her camera and took three different snaps of the man. Then she called to the police motor-cyclist, who was getting off his bike: "Look, he's trying to get into my Dad's car!"

The policeman still had his leather gauntlets on. As he started to push one hand in the window crack to force the glass down, he found that it seemed to slide downwards of its own accord. "Just as though the car was trying to help me," he said afterwards.

The noise of horns had suddenly stopped. The man in the black blazer was jumping up and down and clutching his badly squeezed hand.

"Driving licence, sir?" asked the policeman. The man was too taken up with his damaged hand to answer, so the policeman unbuttoned his blazer. He was very surprised to find in the inside pockets *eight* assorted wallets, each with a different name inside.

He became very suspicious and called for help with his walkie-talkie radio set. A panda car soon arrived and the man in the black blazer was driven away still holding his squeezed hand under his arm.

"Please could we borrow your camera?" asked the police motor-cyclist, "So that the photos you took can be used as evidence against him?"

Maria agreed. What an amazing thing to happen!

"Well done," said the blue car to Slug. "That was pretty quick thinking."

"Don't mention it," said Slug modestly. "And thanks for your help."

Tom and Maria had to go to the police station to explain what had happened; then they all spent the rest of the day on the beach. Much later that evening Slug drove the family home, excited but very tired. Annie made a large pot of tea and sliced some chocolate cake, then Brian carried it all in on a tray. Everyone was exhausted; even Hairy could only flop on to the rug and bury his nose in his paws.

"I'll just see the end of the news, if you don't mind," said Tom, switching on the television.

The announcer was saying: "And here is a pretty amazing last item. A well known pickpocket has at last been arrested by the police, who have been trying to find evidence against him for several months.

"Seaside Sid was actually photographed today by a quick-witted little girl, Maria Mablesden—" ("Hurray!" shouted Brian) "as he attempted to take a purse from her father's car. Somehow his arm got jammed in the open car window, and somehow the horn of the car, and that of the next car, started to sound at the same time, and so the alarm was raised."

"Somehow!" exclaimed Maria. "Slug knew *exactly* what she was doing." Suddenly the newsreader was no longer to be seen on the screen. Instead they saw a blown-up picture of Seaside Sid, his face creased in an expression of intense shock, trying to pull his hand free from Slug's window.

"My photo!" exclaimed Maria.

"My golly!" said Brian.

"My goodness!" said Annie.

"My car!" cried Tom.

But Hairy beat them all. He bounded over to the television set, wagging his tail furiously and barking as loudly as he ever had in his life. *His* car, on *his* television! It was one of Hairy's proudest moments!

4
FATHER'S DAY

———————

"Guess what Sunday is?" said Tom brightly at breakfast time.

"Breakfast-in-bed-brought-up-by-the-children Day," said Annie immediately.

"No," said Tom and Maria and Brian all together.

"International Do-Exactly-What-You-Like Day," suggested Brian.

"No," said Annie and Tom.

"The day you raise our pocket money?" asked Maria hopefully.

"No," they said again.

Hairy stared hopefully at the blank television screen. "Telly Day for Square-Eyed Dogs," suggested Brian.

"No, no, *no!*" said Tom. "Haven't you looked at the calendar? It'll be Father's Day. I'm really looking forward to all the treats and surprises you've got in store for me."

"Huh," said Brian as though he hadn't heard. "Time for school."

"Yes," said Maria. "Come on, or there'll be no time to play before the bell." They both seized their school bags—and were gone.

"I must get that washing into the machine before it rains," said Annie and bustled out into the kitchen.

Tom was left on his own. "You'd think I'd just shouted

'Fire!'" he said. "I only mentioned Father's Day." He stared glumly at Hairy. "Every dog has its day—why can't every father?"

Sunday morning arrived. Tom had completely forgotten what day it was. At seven o'clock the alarm clock went off as usual, by mistake. Annie shot up in bed to turn it off, pulling most of the blankets off Tom as she did so. In her bleary state she knocked the clock on to the floor. It disappeared into the fluff and darkness under the bed, still ringing loudly and making the floor vibrate.

"Quiet!" Annie shouted at it. "You'll wake Tom up, and it's Father's Day: he's having a lie-in." She bent over the edge of the bed, feeling desperately underneath for the clock, which slid away on the slippery lino every time her fingers touched it.

By now her top half was hanging over the edge of the bed, while her legs were still under the blankets, pushing hard against Tom's back, Maria poked her head round the door. "The alarm's going off—" she said unnecessarily, then broke off and stared at her mother. "Gosh, Mum, are you practising for a wheelbarrow race?"

"Sssh," said her mother. "Don't wake your father, he's having a lie-in." The alarm clock burped and stopped. "That's better," said Annie, and pushed herself back into bed, pulling the rest of the blankets off Tom as she did so. He frantically heaved them back again and rolled them into a tight cocoon round himself. Wouldn't they ever let him go back to sleep in this madhouse?

Pad-pad-pad-pad-pad—*thud*!

"YOW-OW-OW!" yelled Tom. Hairy had run upstairs, pushed past Maria and jumped straight up on to him. Tom was now imprisoned in his blanket cocoon, his arms clamped to his sides, quite unable to move and hardly able to breathe.

"Ssssh," said Annie to Tom. "It's Sunday, why don't you have a nice lie-in?"

"WhathyouthinthIthryingthotho?" shouted Tom through a gag of sheets, as Hairy affectionately pawed his face.

"Mind out, Maria," said Brian, coming into the bedroom with a tray. "I thought you'd like your breakfast in bed, Mum, seeing as it's Father's Day."

"Well, it should be breakfast for Dad then," said their mother.

"Oh yes, but he's always so fast asleep in the mornings," said Brian. "I thought you'd enjoy it more." He put the tray on the bedside table. The bed was shaking violently, as Tom, fighting for air, wrestled with Hairy.

"Oh, look, Tom," said Annie. "Isn't Brian a dear?—A mug of . . . er . . . lemonade and some toasted cheese . . ."

"Yes, that's the one I do best at Cubs," said Brian proudly. Then he added in a loud whisper: "Maria and me have a surprise for Dad. We'll give it to him later. We've left it on the television—"

At this magic word Hairy leapt off Tom's heaving body and bounded down the stairs. Tom pushed a beetroot-coloured face above the blankets and gasped in lungfuls of air like a surfacing skin-diver.

"Oh, Tom, you've woken up at last," said Annie. "I thought you might have liked a lie-in this morning. Anyway, now you're awake, would you like some toasted cheese?"

Tom's reply was very muffled and rather ungracious,

so Annie got out of bed, put on her dressing-gown and went out with the tray, shutting the bedroom door firmly behind her.

Much later that day, after a large Sunday lunch, Tom was sitting behind one of his newspapers.

"Er . . . Dad," said Maria. A grunt was heard behind the paper.

"Do you remember what day it is today?" asked Brian. Another grunt.

"It's Father's Day," said Maria, helping Brian out (grunt), "and we didn't quite know what you'd like—"

The newspaper crumpled on to Tom's lap. "Bottle of wine, chocolates, cans of beer, a bottle opener, a corkscrew, a new wallet, a bundle of fivers to put in it—" he said, without drawing breath.

"So we got you this," went on Brian, holding out a very small square parcel.

Tom peered at it in disappointment. "Oh, it's not the bottle of wine, then. But I suppose it might be the new wallet, or even the fivers." He unwrapped it. "—Oh, goodness, what on *earth* is this?"

Lying inside the brown paper was a greenish-white plastic skeleton. "It's a dangler," said Maria.

"With a suction pad," nodded Brian.

"You hang it in your car," explained Maria.

"We thought it might brighten Slug up a bit inside," said Brian. "It's luminous, so you can see it shining when you're driving in the dark."

Tom picked it up cautiously by the string. The skeleton clicked its bony heels together politely and dangled its long legs and arms.

"If there's one thing I need as I drive along in the dark," said Tom, "it's a luminous skelly."

Hairy thought he said "telly" and leapt over to him and licked his face gratefully.

"*No*, Hairy, I am *not* going to switch it on," said Tom. "In fact, I'm going outside to hang this inside Slug."

The Father's Day skelly was the beginning of a large collection intended to make Slug look more interesting inside and out. For their mother's birthday Maria and Brian bought another dangler: two large dice made of green fluffy material with great black spots. The dice dangled in the back window, while the skelly jigged up and down below the mirror at the front.

When they went on holiday they collected stickers from every place they visited. Soon the side windows were covered with coloured squares and triangles. "It's like a blessed church in here," grumbled Grandma when they gave her a lift one day. "All these stained glass windows. You need something more cheerful to brighten you up a bit."

The next thing the family knew, Grandma had brought a stick-on vase with a bright purple wax rose to stand in it. "I thought it was just the thing for Slug's inside," she said. "Specially as it came free with my soap flakes." She insisted on sticking it in the middle of the dashboard, so that every time Tom wanted to see how much petrol he had left, he had to push aside prickly waxen rose leaves. It was even more of a nuisance when he bent over to pull out the choke and hooked his glasses on the spiky rose petals.

Then Annie bought a sticker for Slug's back mud-guard. "It's for those chaps who follow so close behind us that they roar down poor little Slug's exhaust pipe," she explained. In tiny lettering it read:

"If you can read this, you are too close."

In the next few weeks there was no stopping Maria and
Brian. They pounced on every single thing that was bought
and brought into the house, removing all sticky labels and
re-sticking them on Slug's windows or insides. It became a
family craze—until Grandma, unintentionally, put a stop
to it.

She arrived one morning flushed and triumphant, and
emptied her bag onto the table. A pile of large yellow
sticky letters fell out:

M B A D A R M U A R A N D I M I

"The man in the Car Boutique said that once they were
stuck on, they were stuck as tight as the nose on your
face."

The children stared blankly.

"Don't you see?" she asked impatiently. "Two names
on the front windscreen and two on the back: MUM DAD
and MARIA BRIAN."

The children looked at her with new respect; they
hadn't thought of that one. They went straight out and
worked inside Slug for half an hour, Brian at the front and
Maria at the back. It was rather tricky, as the words had to
be stuck on like mirror writing, so that they looked the
right way round from outside.

Hairy whined on irritatingly as they worked, so when
they'd finished, they took him in and settled down to
watch Bugs Bunny with him.

Ten minutes later they heard Tom's voice: "Maria?
Brian?" He burst into the room. "Who stuck the writing
on the car?" he roared.

"Don't you think they're great, Dad?" asked Brian
brightly.

"And Grandma says they're stuck as tight as the nose on
your face," said Maria. Tom's face looked even blacker.

Annie came running into the house. "Have you seen the car?" she shrieked. "Guess what they've stuck on the front window!"

"MUM and DAD," said Maria. "That's nice."

"No!" roared Tom.

"No!" shrieked Annie. "In big letters for all the world to see, it says DUM and MAD!"

Brian and Maria looked horrified, then caught one another's eye and collapsed in helpless giggles on top of Hairy who was lying across their laps.

"You *silly* children," roared Tom—He caught Annie's eye, and he too started to smile, then chortle, as he saw the funny side of it. "But that's the finish," he warned. "Not another sticker or dangler goes on that car, or we'll need a periscope to see what's happening outside. So remember —that's the finish."

Annie wiped her eyes and added, "And as for the person who stuck MARIA and BRAIN on the back window—she needs *her* brain examined."

"Oh!" Maria was mortified; that wretched mirror writing. "Shall I go and change it round?" she mumbled.

"No, they're stuck as tight as the nose on your face," said Tom and Annie together.

"Can't we just leave it as it is? After all, *I* don't mind a bit . . . !" smirked "Brain".

5
TROUBLE WITH A DUMMY

———◆———

Grandma was sitting upright on a hard wooden chair, swathed in bandages. Both her legs were tightly bound to splints; one arm was also bandaged to a splint and the other was in a sling. Her head and jaw were encased in white too. The only spots of colour were her two brightly flushed cheeks and her delphinium-blue hat. She had insisted that Maria place the hat back on her head the moment the fractured-skull bandage was in place.

Maria stood back and looked at her grandmother. "You look great, Grandma—just like something from a horror film."

"Oh, thanksh," said Grandma stiffly. The chin bandage made speech very difficult.

"I'm sure I'll get my first aid badge," said Maria, "don't you think so, Grandma?" Her grandmother grunted and flickered her eyelids—even nodding her head was tricky.

At that moment Annie came in with the tablecloth, saw her mother and screamed. "Mother! What *has* happened? Maria, why didn't you tell me? I didn't know there'd been an accident."

"There hashn't," said Grandma through tight lips.

"It's my first aid, Mum," explained Maria. "You know I want my Brownie badge. Grandma's been letting me practise on her."

Annie had sunk on to the settee, dabbing her horror-struck face with the tablecloth. "*Maria*," she exclaimed. "You might have warned me. Grandma looks like something from *The Mummy's Curse*."

"Thanksh again," muttered Grandma. "Ishn't it tibe I had by tea?"

"Yes, of course it is, Mother," said Annie soothingly, and laid the cloth over the table. "Maria! Unwind poor Grandma!"

"I can't find the end," wailed Maria, walking round and round her grandmother, peering at the tangle of criss-crossed bandages. It took fifteen minutes before Grandma was completely untied and she was able to rub the circulation back into her numb arms and legs.

"I'll just sip my tea gently," she said, waving away the cake plate. "I think my jaws have forgotten how to open and close properly."

"This is ridiculous, Maria," said her mother. "Can't you practise on Brian? Or your dolls? You can't carry on tying people to chairs like a gangster."

"But I've got to have real live people to practise on," said Maria. "Brown Owl said we had to."

Her mother pressed her lips together. "You children always take things to such extremes," she said.

The next day when Brian and Maria came home from school, Annie was obviously pleased with herself. "Guess who I saw today," she said as she filled the kettle.

"Toyah."

"Prince Andrew."

"No—Uncle Jack."

"Oh, but he's not special," said Brian in disappointment.

"I never said he was special," said their mother, "but he happened to mention that they were getting rid of some of their old stock and shop fittings at The Elegant Emporium. Do you know, they've still got some cash registers at the back of that shop that ring up pounds, shillings and pence!"

"But we don't want a cash register, do we?"

"Of course not, silly, but guess what else Uncle Jack was trying to get rid of?—A very old tailor's dummy!"

There was silence as the children took this in. "Why do we want one of them?" asked Maria at last.

"Well, I thought eventually it would be useful for me to use as a dressmaker's dummy to hang clothes on when I'm sewing. But for *now* I thought you could use it for practising first aid, Maria."

Maria thought about it. "Mmm, but Brown Owl said—"

"Never mind Brown Owl," said her mother firmly. "If she'd seen Grandma bandaged like the Mummy's Curse, she'd—"

"Oh, all right then," agreed Maria hastily. "Is Uncle Jack bringing it over?"

"Oh no, I said you'd go over with your Dad one evening and fetch it."

It was dusk as Tom and the children drove up to Uncle Jack's shop, The Elegant Emporium. The main doors were closed and the assistants had gone home. Uncle Jack was waiting for them at the side entrance in a narrow dark alley. "Just come inside for a moment and see if the dummy's suitable, will you?" he suggested. "It's in the store room next door."

As they entered, their uncle switched on a very dim light, but the rest of the store stretched away into the darkness. Odd shapes loomed out of the gloom where white dustcovers hid the displays. "Isn't it spooky?" whispered Brian.

"Don't be silly," said Maria, looking nervously into the dim corners of the shop. The two children went towards the store room which Uncle Jack had pointed out to them. Suddenly they both gasped and moved closer together. Except for a weak light from a street lamp, the store room was in dark shadow. Directly in front of the children stood a tall, white, hollow-eyed figure, pale as ivory and pointing one bony finger straight at them.

"Gosh," whispered Brian, his eyes wide. "She's got nothing on!"

"Oh dear," said Maria. "We'll have to find her a blanket or something." In a few moments the two men appeared.

"Oh," said Tom, taken aback. "She's certainly a big lady to get in our car, Jack."

"Look, Tom, you've got your roof rack on," said Uncle Jack. "She'll be all right on there. Here's this old bit of carpeting from Furnishings. We'll wrap it round her and then you can tie her on. How about that?" He rolled the piece of carpeting round the model and they tied it round her middle and ankles with string from Hardware.

"It's that pointing arm," complained Tom, wrinkling his nose thoughtfully and pushing his spectacles up. "That's going to look a bit odd on the car roof."

"Oh, don't fuss, Tom," said Uncle Jack. He wanted to lock up and get home. After all, he was giving them a perfectly good tailor's dummy *and* a piece of carpeting (not to mention the string from Hardware) *free*. How they got home was their problem.

The two men lifted the rolled-up dummy on to the roof rack and tied her down across her legs and her neck. Her arm pointed accusingly up at the moon, which was just appearing from behind the clouds.

"Cheers, Jack," called Tom, as they all climbed into Slug. "Thanks very much."

As they drove away from the dark side door of The Elegant Emporium, they were spotted by a strolling couple. "Look at those feet sticking out of that roll of carpet. Rex, they're feet, *human* feet. Someone's tried to hide a body in a roll of carpet!"

"Oh, get on with you, Aggie! You read too many thrillers."

"Oh, Rex, look, it's rolling from side to side on the top of the car, and it's managed to get a hand free from its bonds. Look at that naked arm—it's waving for help, Rex. It's still alive!"

"OK, OK, I've got the car number—it certainly looks suspicious."

They ran to the nearest phone box and alerted the police. It was a quiet evening at the police station, and this sounded like a brutal case of kidnapping. Two police cars were soon within sight of Slug, rattling along at a steady twenty-five miles an hour. The kidnapped victim still had an arm free, and waved beseechingly for help every time the car jolted.

As the little white car lurched to a halt at the Mablesdens' front gate, the two police cars with sirens wailing converged on it. With a slamming of doors which made several neighbours rush to their windows, the policemen ran over to Slug. "Could we see what you've got tied to your roof, sir?" said an officer sternly to Tom.

"On my roof?" blinked Tom, looking up at his house. "Oh—you mean on the roof of the *car*. Yes, of course you can, but it's only a roll of carpet—" But the policemen were already untying the cruel bonds which tied the victim down.

The neighbours' eyes widened as the four policemen carefully stood the roll of carpet upright on the pavement. Very gently one of them unrolled it: they didn't know what state the kidnapped victim would be in. An ambulance with blaring siren drew up behind Slug and the police cars. The two ambulance men ran forward to give assistance to the group of policemen. The neighbours were now standing in groups in their doorways, anxious not to miss anything.

All eyes were on the roll of carpet. The ambulance driver was trying to feel the pulse on the wrist of the pointing arm. He shook his head: "Stone cold," he said sadly. The carpet sagged slowly to the pavement, and they all stared at the stiff, cold-looking female body which stood there. Her feet were unable to balance on the uneven paving stones and she ve-ery slowly fell back into the arms of a tall policeman.

"Poor soul, she must be perished," muttered Mr Fastnet, peering out into the street.

"Fainted from exposure," nodded Mrs Fastnet.

"Hypothermia," agreed her husband, still staring at the scene outside the Mablesdens' gate.

The tall policeman half-carried, half-trundled the stiff, naked lady into Number Nine, followed by the other policemen with the carpet, the ambulance men, Tom and the children. The front door shut behind them and the neighbours were left with only Slug to look at.

Suddenly, they heard an explosion from inside Number Nine. The walls shook and the windows rattled as ten people roared with laughter. The mystery had been explained.

Hairy liked to see everyone enjoying themselves, so he started to bark happily too. The noise was unbelievable. The white lady was still leaning rather drunkenly against the dining room wall, pointing straight at the front door, when the bell rang.

"Oh dear, oh dear, oh dear," chuckled the ambulance driver, wiping his eyes, "I've been on some odd errands, but never one like this . . ." He opened the front door. There stood kind little Mrs Fastnet with a steaming bowl in her hands.

"I thought perhaps some hot broth . . . ?" she faltered. Then she saw the tall white figure staring straight at her and pointing accusingly. "Aaaagh," she shrieked.

The ambulance man caught the bowl of broth just in time and led Mrs Fastnet gently into the living room to explain. Soon her husband was ringing at the door to enquire after his wife, and he was taken in to enjoy the joke. Next came Mr and Mrs Rockall, and finally the curious Mallin sisters. Everybody enjoyed the story, and nobody thought of refusing when Tom brought out his best home-made beetroot wine.

It was nearly midnight when the guests regretfully decided to go home. The white lady leant against the wall and showed them the way out with a long white finger. "Best party I've been to in years," said Mr Fastnet, bowing over her cold hand as they said their Goodbyes.

Maria got her first aid badge easily, of course. Brown Owl said she must have done hours of practice on someone.

"Oh no," said Maria. "My patient was a model."

"You mean you had a model patient?" said Brown Owl.

"Well, yes, sort of . . ."

6

HAIRY THE TELLY HOUND

———— • ————

It was July. Every afternoon there was tennis from Wimbledon on the television. It was Hairy's favourite part of the summer. Maria and Brian were at school all day and Tom was at work. Hairy and Annie could sit in peace the whole afternoon watching the tennis.

Hairy liked his bowl of water placed near the television set. Whenever the players changed ends and had a drink and a rub with a towel, Hairy too would walk sedately to his bowl, have a drink, rub his ears against Annie's easy chair and go to the other end of the rug, refreshed and ready for the next game.

One afternoon while they watched, the room was lit up by a flash of lightning. Annie got up and looked outside. The sky had become very dark and the trees and bushes started to wave violently to and fro. Cra-a-a-ack! The thunder boomed across the dark sky. Huge drops of rain as big as ten pence pieces splashed on to the ground, and it began to pour. Leaves and flowers bent over, little puddles of mud formed in the flowerbeds.

"It's raining cats and dogs out there," said Annie. Hairy pricked up his ears and went to stare out of the window. After a while he decided that it didn't look as exciting outside as Annie had suggested, so he gave her a disappointed glance.

Cra-a-a-ack! Boom! Ziz-ziz-ziz! Lightning and thunder seemed to flash and boom together. The tennis commentary stopped and the screen went blank.

"Oh, darn and botheration," said Annie. "It's the weather—it's playing tricks with the telly." And to Hairy's dismay she turned the knob marked OFF.

Then she went into the kitchen to get tea ready and listen to a radio commentary from Wimbledon. Hairy found himself all alone with only a dark screen to look at. There was worse to come. When Tom returned home from work, he fiddled about with the controls, then wound up all the flex, staggered outside with the set and placed it in the boot of the car.

"I'll leave it at Ted's in the morning," he said. "He'll soon have it working again."

Hairy couldn't believe his eyes. *His* television set was being left out there in the dark boot of the car, when *he* could have been lying on the rug in front of it having a long evening's viewing. He climbed up on the chair next to the window and stared out stonily. He saw Brian and Maria run up and down outside, but took no notice.

"Tea-time, Hairy," called Annie, but again he took no notice. *His* telly was sitting out there in that silly white car at the kerbside, and it looked like staying there all night.

"I think he's sulking," said Annie in a low voice. "He's not forgiven me for turning off the telly when it broke down."

"Come on, Hairy," called Brian. "Let's go walkies." Hairy didn't move a muscle, and continued to stare through the window. He stayed there the whole evening, refusing all food. In the end Brian and Maria had to go to bed, and even then Hairy didn't come upstairs to get in the way and play hide and seek under the beds or hunt-the-socks as he usually did.

Suddenly there was pandemonium downstairs. Hairy was barking at the top of his voice and racing from Tom and Annie to the front door and back. Then he was scrabbling madly at the door with his front paws and barking again at Tom and Annie. "What on earth's the matter, Hairy?" asked Annie, "Shush, *shush!*"

Brian and Maria were calling over the banisters from the landing: "What's the matter with Hairy?"

Tom couldn't stand the noise a moment longer and opened the front door to let the nearly hysterical dog out. "Oh, NO!" he shouted. He stood in the doorway unable to believe his eyes.

Brian was first downstairs and pushed past his father. "Oh, NO," he shouted too. "Slug's gone. Slug's GONE. Maria, Mum, Slug's GONE!"

Tom ran to the kerbside to look up and down the street, but there was no sign of the little white car. Annie and the two children stood in the doorway and watched as Tom ran to the other corner of the street where the phone box stood. In a moment he was inside. "He'll be phoning the police," said Annie.

"Where's Hairy?" asked Maria.

"No sign of him," said her mother. "He just raced out of the front door and streaked away down the street. He must have seen Slug being driven away and that's why he started to bark."

"Clever old Hairy," said Brian.

"Oh, I hope he's all right," said Maria rather tearfully. "Suppose it's burglars, with masks on, and—"

"No, no," said her mother. "I'm sure Hairy can look after himself."

Hairy was still streaking along the streets, following Slug. He was just managing to keep the little white car within sight. Slug was not co-operating with her driver, a boy of about seventeen. His mate sat next to him.

"Come on, Jammer, step on it. I thought you said it would be a joy-ride? More like a pram-ride, this is!"

"Who asked for your opinions, Fatso? *You* can't even drive. You just watch out for the fuzz."

Fatso half turned round and watched the road behind. "Nothing in sight except a dog."

"Great. Now I'll try and get some speed out of this old tin can." But Jammer didn't know how stubborn Slug could be. Besides, she was due for a visit to Mr Fortescue's petrol station for a fill-up and so felt very sluggish indeed. She started to grumble and stutter and choke, and her engine groaned and she began to jump and bounce—and finally she stalled. Slug had stopped dead.

"A joy-ride. A joy-ride?" shouted Fatso mockingly. "Trust you to pick an older banger with no guts. I told you to go for a Jag."

"Whaddya mean?" demanded Jammer. "Whose idea was it to see if the driver's door was open, anyway?" As the two boys sat there getting more and more angry with one another, Hairy caught up with them and started to bark. He stood on the pavement with sharp white teeth bared. When he stood and barked menacingly like that, at the top of his voice, Hairy could look very big and frightening indeed.

"Shut him up, can't you?" said Fatso, "or half the street will be coming out to see what's going on." Jammer half opened the door, then shut it again quickly as Hairy bounded round at him. Fatso opened his door and started to get out. Hairy shot round Slug's bonnet and fastened his teeth on Fatso's plump ankle.

"Ow-aaghhh!" shrieked Fatso, and tried to pull the door smartly shut. It slammed hard on his own leg and he shrieked again: "Ow-aaaghhh!"

"Shut up," yelled Jammer, and panicked. He leapt out of his door and started to run. Hairy let go of Fatso's ankle and galloped after Jammer. He was growling at Jammer's ankles as they reached the corner of the street, and there, cruising towards them, came a neat little panda police car . . .

Much later that night Tom and Hairy drove back home again in Slug. One of the policemen had fetched Tom a gallon can of petrol from Mr Fortescue's. "Slug playing up *again*, is she?" tutted Mr Fortescue, when he was told what it was for.

Maria and Brian had stayed up in their pyjamas, waiting to hear news of Hairy. Maria was the first to spot Slug lurching round the corner of the street. "There they are!" she shouted. "And there's Hairy, sitting next to Dad."

"Hurray," shouted Brian. "He's safe!"

"Yes, good old Tom," said their mother.

"No, good old Hairy, I mean," said Brian.

They all made a tremendous fuss of Hairy and gave him a huge supper. "Aren't you a *clever* Hairy!" said Maria, hugging him tightly. But Hairy wasn't interested. He was scratching again at the front door, and when they opened it, he raced down the path to Slug. He walked round and round the car, whining and sniffing, then seated himself squarely beside the door of the boot.

"What on earth is the matter with that dog?" demanded Tom. "We've got the car back, thanks to him, what more does he want?"

"I think he wants the boot open," suggested Brian.

Tom sighed heavily and went down the path to unlock Slug's boot. "Wowrrrow-rrow-rrrow-ow!" barked Hairy in a frenzy of happiness. He jumped up and down and got his paws inside the boot, patting the television set lovingly. "Rrrowwrrowruff!" he barked, gazing devotedly at the square screen.

"He's just inspecting Slug to make sure she's not been damaged inside or out," Tom explained to the others.

"Amazing . . ." breathed Annie admiringly.

"Rubbish!" growled Hairy to Slug. "I'm not bothered about a heap of scrap metal—I'm checking that my telly's OK!"

7

THE CARNIVAL

———◆———

Grandma was in one of her organizing moods. "I think you should *all* be in the next carnival procession," she said. "I could soon run up a pretty little costume for Maria—do you fancy being a bluebell, dear? Or a pink velvet rose? And Brian—you could be a page-boy, strewing flower-petals in the procession. Now how about it?"

The horrified expressions on the children's faces soon told Grandma what they thought of that bright idea. "Oh," she said, and looked disappointed for a few minutes. Then a new idea occurred to her. "What about a float? Slug could be covered in flowers. Think of that: she could glide forward like a swan, smothered in blossoms!" Grandma clasped her hands together and closed her eyes, imagining this beauteous sight.

Hairy sat up and howled; the thought of covering that old tin can with flowers was more than he could bear. Grandma blinked and looked at him. "Oh, I do believe Hairy wants to be part of it too. *You* could have a coat of . . . of dog daisies, Hairy, or . . . dog roses or something."

She turned to the children. "I've masses of flowers in my garden. I could make him something sweetly pretty, you know."

Maria didn't think that anything could make Hairy into

a sweetly pretty dog, but she was so relieved at not having to be a bluebell herself that she didn't dare object.

"That's settled then," said Grandma. "I'll talk to your father about making a frame to cover Slug (except her windscreen, of course, or she couldn't be driven). Then we'll fix flowers to the framework the night before the carnival procession. And we'll make some sort of costume for Hairy too, so he won't feel left out—will you, old boy?" She patted Hairy encouragingly and he howled with dismay at what was coming.

Tom wasn't too keen on Grandma's ideas. He knew they usually meant plenty of work for other people—under Grandma's supervision. "Most people are workers," she would say, with a faraway look in her eyes, "but only a few can bring a spark of originality—and I can modestly claim to be one of those few." She thought and talked of nothing but the Carnival for a whole week.

"Slug is to be a white swan—as I suggested. We'll smother her with white flowers!" (Tom had the impossible task of making a long, graceful swan's neck out of rabbit-hutch wire. It was to be fixed to Slug's roof and bonnet, somehow.)

Grandma went on: "And as Hairy doesn't want to be left out, he shall be a white cygnet, swimming gracefully behind his mother. If Tom drives Slug at about three miles per hour, it should look as though the two of them are gliding along . . ."

"But how can Hairy swim behind?" objected Maria. "He usually gallops everywhere."

"I've thought of that too," said Grandma, her eyes sparkling. "We'll put him on your go-kart, Brian, and tie the front of it to Slug's back bumper—so the mother swan will pull her little cygnet along behind her. Can't you just picture it?"

Soon Hairy had had several costume fittings. He was to wear a sort of white dust-sheet which would cover him completely except for his eyes and a nose-hole. A light-weight cygnet's neck (made of rabbit-hutch wire) was to be fitted to his head, and then the whole thing—costume and neck and head—was to be covered in white flowers.

The children had told him that he would just have to lie still inside his cygnet's costume and be pulled along by Slug. "It'll be a lovely ride, Hairy," said Brian coaxingly. "And we'll even smuggle a meaty bone inside your costume; you'll have a great time."

Hairy thought differently. The whole thing sounded ridiculous. He didn't like having that white sheet all over him—or that wire contraption on his head. (And if they *wanted* a young swan, he knew there was a family of five of them living down in the flooded gravel pits.) Nor did he like the idea of being pulled along by Slug. "She'll fancy herself, having *me* trailing behind, at her mercy, the whole afternoon. It would be just like her to pull me over all the bumps and holes in the road . . . And think of all the television I'll miss. It's on a Saturday afternoon—all that sport!"

But Slug wasn't looking forward to the carnival either. "Me—a swan? Aw, go on!" she thought, when Brian and Maria told her what was in store for her. Then they told her about the part Hairy was to play, and she became even more indignant. "Me, pull that hairy specimen?" she spluttered to herself. "What's wrong with his own four legs anyway? Besides—whoever heard of a swan on four legs, *or* on wheels, come to that?"

But Grandma's bee was well and truly in her bonnet, and no matter how much Hairy might yowl or Slug might turn down the corners of her radiator grille, they were going to have to take part.

On the afternoon before the carnival, Hairy managed to slink out of the house unnoticed. Slug was parked next to the kerb. Hairy went round to her other side, which couldn't be seen from the house. He wasted no time.

"Something's got to be done."

"I quite agree!" snapped Slug. "The whole business is getting out of hand." She was so angry that her mirrors were misting up.

"When are they dressing you up?" asked Hairy.

"This evening," spluttered Slug. "They're going to park me in that field next to Grandma's garden, then it will be easy to pick the flowers and stick them on my . . . *frame*, ready for tomorrow. A swan! I ask you—has any other solid, reliable family car ever been so humiliated . . . ?"

Hairy was thinking hard. "I've an idea," he said. "Pretend you're playing along with them. Drive Tom to Grandma's as sweetly as you can—don't let him think there's anything bothering you. Got that?"

"I'll try," gritted Slug. "But you'd better have some darned good idea to get me out of this farce, or you'll never ride in me again!"

"Don't worry," soothed Hairy. "Just park in that field, let them dress you up—it's miles from any roads your friends use, so no one's likely to see you. Then wait, and see what happens."

"Don't let me down," begged Slug. Hairy mooched back into the house.

.That evening Slug bravely rattled round country lanes to Grandma's cottage. Tom got out, opened the gate into the field alongside the cottage garden, and parked Slug in the corner. Hairy had been sitting very quietly with the children in the back. When they got out, he slipped between their legs, and they didn't notice him streaking across to the neighbouring field. He wanted a word with the goats who grazed there.

Tom, Grandma and the children worked very hard all evening. They fixed on Slug's wire framework. The tall neck and swan's head and beak (painted by Maria) were very impressive. Grandma pinned the white cloth in position, so that Slug was completely draped in white, with only her windscreen hole and the lower half of her four wheels showing.

"There!" said Grandma. "Now I'll fetch the white flowers—I've got basketfuls—and what a beautiful swan she'll be!"

She was right. When the two-hour task was completed, Slug had been transformed into a beautiful white swan, whose graceful neck and head rose high above her bonnet. She was covered in white flowers and looked a picture. In fact, Tom took some colour photos of the Slug-swan. "Lovely," he said. "Perhaps your idea wasn't so bad after all, Mother, I bet she wins a prize tomorrow."

They all went into the cottage for some supper. This was the moment Hairy had been waiting for. "Come on, you greedy goats," he growled. "Through that hole in the hedge. Over there, just waiting for you, are the tastiest mouthfuls you've ever had. And I'm letting you have them all to yourselves."

He pushed his way through the hedge and the four goats scrambled eagerly after him. "Baa-aa!" they said, and their hungry yellow eyes lit up as they spotted the juicy blossoms all over the Slug-swan. "Baa-aa!" they cried and trotted across.

"Keep still!" hissed Hairy to Slug. "Your troubles will soon be over."

The goats were most obliging. They nibbled the white daisies and the white carnations. They gulped down mouthfuls of white roses (they didn't seem to notice the prickles). They stood on their hind legs, stretched up and pulled at the white blossoms on the swan's neck and wings. Everything edible they ate.

When they had finished, the swan looked very bedraggled. It had dirty hoofprints all over it, and every one of its blossom-feathers had disappeared. Even the neck dipped down to the ground, since the goats in their eagerness had pulled at the framework with their strong teeth.

When Grandma came out of her cottage for one last look, her screams nearly shattered Slug's windscreen. "Those goats," she screamed. "Those horrible goats! They've *ruined* our swan. Ruined it! And how did they get in, I'd like to know. Who let them in?"

Of course, no one thought of Hairy, who was nowhere to be seen anyway. Tom helped Grandma into the cottage. After a medicinal glass of brandy, she felt more her old self.

"Right then," she said firmly, her eyes even more glazed with determination (or possibly brandy) than before. "Perhaps swans *were* a little ambitious—we'll think of something else. And tomorrow we'll concentrate on Hairy, he's our only hope now. Agreed? Agreed."

Hairy had no idea what was in store for him. When Maria whistled, he came running obediently from the rose garden, as innocently as though he'd spent the afternoon

enjoying the fragrance of the flowers. Now he hoped it
would be telly-time.

Slug hissed through the hedge: "Thanks, old man."

"That's OK," said Hairy gruffly. "I guess they'll call it
off now."

He couldn't have been more wrong!

Grandma wouldn't let him anywhere near the television. The others pushed and pulled him upstairs to the
bathroom, where Tom and Maria and Brian *lifted* him,
howling loudly in protest, into a warm bath. They soaped
him down and brushed him and rinsed him, until his thick
fur was shining clean, and its mixture of colours gleamed
with health.

"Yee-ooooow-ow-oww!" he howled, lifting his nose
despairingly.

"Now get to bed all of you," ordered Grandma.

Hairy curled up in his basket and shuddered with
dread. What would that awful woman think up next? He
had a restless night, twitching in his sleep as hissing swans
flew at him in his dreams.

The next morning Grandma was in great form. "It's all
decided," she announced triumphantly. "We'll have to
leave Slug out of our reckoning now, thanks to those evil
goats, and I think we'll have to leave out Brian too—
awfully sorry, dear." Brian's eyes lit up with relief. "We'll
concentrate on Hairy instead," said Grandma.

Hairy's heart sank to his paws. He wished he could
crawl under the carpet and be forgotten, just for Carnival
Day, but Grandma was continuing: "Yes, Maria, you're
to be *Mary*—now that's suitable, isn't it? And Hairy is to
be your little lamb. You know—'Mary had a little lamb,
its fleece was white as snow, and everywhere that Mary
went, the lamb was sure to go.'"

"Lamb? Me?" thought Hairy. Was the woman completely off her rocker?

"Hairy's not as white as snow," pointed out Maria. "He's sort of pepper and salt and mustard all mixed up."

"Oh, but we can soon alter all that," said Grandma, with a gay little laugh that made Hairy cringe even more. "We'll simply smother him with flour. I've a three-pound bag of self-raising and a three-pound bag of plain—that should be enough to make a lamb of him."

"He's a bit big for a lamb," ventured Brian.

"Well, size is relative, isn't it?" said Grandma grandly, and that was settled.

The hour of the carnival procession wore on. Maria was dressed in her best red dress. "Look, I've sewn lots of red frills round the hem," said Grandma. "And with your little red kerchief over your head, you'll look quite like a young Victorian miss walking to school. You can carry this basket of posies to complete the picture." She stood back, beaming at a resigned Maria.

"Oh, *sweetly* pretty," said Grandma, clasping her hands together. "What do you think, Brian?"

Brian couldn't answer. He was still sneezing after shaking a whole bag of flour over a snarling, protesting Hairy, who was standing on the garden path, his floury tail between his floury legs. A kind of misty cloud surrounded his whole body, and whenever he sneezed, another few thousand specks of self-raising flour jerked into the air.

"Lovely!" said Grandma. "Now let's all get into Slug—carefully now—and we'll join the procession. It leaves the Town Hall at ten."

Tom drove slowly into town and parked in the car park near the Town Hall. There they all disembarked. "I'm really awfully sorry, old chap," murmured Slug to Hairy.

"I didn't know things would turn out like this." Hairy was too miserable even to snarl.

The procession was lining up in the square in front of the Town Hall, and Grandma soon found Maria and Hairy their place. "Here you are, dears: this section is 'Nursery Rhyme or Fairy Tale.'" They were in front of Humpty Dumpty and behind Puss in Boots.

"Stand still, Hairy," commanded Grandma, and she pulled from her handbag the three-pound bag of plain flour and strewed it freely all over Hairy. Now he looked like a walking snow drift.

"Best of luck, Mary—and your little lamb," hissed Grandma, giving the thumbs up sign. Then she disappeared into the crowd.

The music struck up. The procession moved slowly along the streets. Maria and Hairy moved slowly with it, their faces downcast, their footsteps mournful. As they passed the judges' platform, Hairy sneezed yet again, and flour flew in all directions. Maria moved a few paces away from him, with a horrified look on her face—at least he could keep that flour off her best dress. Hairy drew back his lips ferociously and snarled at his own misfortune; he'd never felt so miserable in his life. There was football, cricket, darts, ice-hockey and snooker on the box this afternoon—and he was missing it all!

Two and a half hours later the judges moved along the length of the procession. Maria couldn't believe her ears when one of them came up to her. "We've seldom seen such a terrified Red Riding Hood and such a ferocious wolf," he said. "You both thoroughly deserve your prize." And he handed her a voucher for five pounds.

"But—" began Maria. Then Hairy sneezed three times and everyone scattered in a cloud of flour. So Maria kept the prize, not quite understanding how they came to win it.

"Bet there's nothing in it for me, though," thought Hairy gloomily. He was right. A sudden summer shower pelted down and brought the carnival to a hasty end. It took the family well into the night to remove the thick coating of flour-and-water paste from Hairy's matted fur.

"Poor lamb," murmured Grandma.

8
SLUG'S LAST FLING

———•———

"Dad, can we go and get some chips?" asked Maria casually one evening.

"Sure," said Tom vaguely, fishing in his pocket for some change and putting a pile of coins into her outstretched hand.

Maria blinked and looked at Brian doubtfully, then back at her father again. "Oh, Dad, are you sure? There's too much here—" she began.

"Can we get a bottle of pop as well?" asked Brian.

"Sure," said their father once more. He began to feel absent-mindedly in his pocket for more money, but they left him hurriedly and went into the kitchen. Their mother was ironing.

"What's got into Dad?" asked Maria. "He's giving all his money away."

"He's not quite himself today," Annie explained. "It's the time of year."

"June?" said Maria, puzzled. "But his birthday's not till October."

"It's not *his* age he's worried about, it's Slug's. She has to have her Ministry of Transport test next Monday morning, and she's getting on a bit, you know. Ten years is a long life for a car, and Slug's several years older than that; she's quite an old lady, really."

"What happens if she fails her test?" asked Brian anxiously.

"We-ell . . ." began Annie doubtfully. They watched her swerving the point of the iron in a slalem round the buttons on a shirt. Then she put the iron on its stand and looked straight at the children. "I suppose you're both old enough to know: they can give Slug a really thorough overhaul and mend any parts that can be repaired. But if that's still no good, then it's the finish for Slug—the end of the road." She lowered her voice. ". . . The scrap-yard . . ."

"Oh!" exclaimed Brian and Maria. It would be awful if anything happened to Slug. How would the family manage without her?

They walked home thoughtfully from the fish and chip shop. Maria held the scrumple of newspaper in her left hand and they took it in turns to dive into the bag and choose a chip. "The scrunchy scraps are best," remarked Maria, poking into the corner of the bag.

"No, I like the long fat ones," said her brother, wiping one round the top of the bag to find the remaining drops of vinegar.

"Poor old Slug," he said suddenly.

"Poor old Dad," said Maria. "And poor all of us! We'll all be lost without Slug."

"We ought to go somewhere special with her before she has her M.O.T. test," said Brian, breathing in gasps of cold air to cool an extra hot chip. "Let's ask Dad."

Maria searched for the last crunchy pieces in the corner of the bag. She rolled the greasy papers into a ball and threw them in the dustbin as they went up the path. "Ugh, look, my hands are all black from the newspaper. What do you mean: 'somewhere special'?"

"Well, like a . . . an outing, or something. While she's still . . . with us."

"Yes—a Last Fling," nodded Maria.

Annie and Tom agree to the idea, and they decided on a day in the country. "It'd better be Saturday then," said Tom, "because on Monday Slug has an important appointment . . ." They all looked at one another, but nothing more was said.

They packed bags and bottles in the boot, Slug breathed in deeply, and they clambered in. Slug's springs protested, her mudguards sagged and her tyres flattened very slightly under the pressure. "Now for the dog-shaped straw that breaks the camel's back," she thought.

"Come on, Hairy," yelled Brian.

Hairy looked up from the crater he was digging in the rosebed for his latest bone. They daren't go without him! He snatched up the bone in his teeth, bounded across the muddy rosebed, raced over the soggy lawn and threw himself, bone first, into the back of the car. Slug bounced up and down on her springs. They slammed the doors. Her engine spluttered crossly into life and they were off.

Tom took an unfamiliar route through the town and soon wished he hadn't. "Oh, look," cried Maria in horrified tones, staring out of her window. "Look at that scrap-yard!" They were passing a long rusty corrugated-iron fence on which was painted in garish green letters: SAM'S SCRAP. Behind the fence they could see huge towers of brokendown car skeletons, piled higgledy-piggledy, twisted and deformed. "It's horrible," said Maria. "It's a cars' graveyard."

"And look what they do to the bodies," said Annie, pointing to another great pile of scrap they were passing. Each car body had been pressed by some giant machine — like a great hand squeezing scraps of silver paper — into a neat cube of tightly compressed layers of metal.

Brian looked shocked: "Fancy letting your car end up like that!"

"Oh, Slug, we *won't*," said Annie, stroking the dash-board affectionately.

After that they were all glad to leave the town behind and jolt slowly through the countryside. "There's a good place!" said Annie suddenly. On one side of the road they could see a green and flowery slope stretching up towards the sky. On the other side, the ground dropped gently to a field where a silvery stream splashed beneath willow trees.

"Oh, that's lovely," said Maria. "Can we stop, Dad?" Tom had already slowed Slug down, and now he backed her to the edge of the road as he usually did, with her little square nose pointing in the direction they would leave by.

Hairy scrabbled out first, then the children and then their parents. As they unloaded everything, Slug seemed to rise several centimetres off her springs with relief. "It's rather muddy just there," said Tom doubtfully, walking round three sides of Slug to make sure she was on firm ground. "There's a patch of mud under her back wheels, but I think she'll be all right."

They had a lovely afternoon. Brian and Maria climbed to the top of the hill first and played Bronze Age men defending their hill-fort against attackers. Hairy had to pretend to be their cattle. He didn't really understand about being rounded up and always wanted to go charging down the hill again. "Perhaps the stampeding cattle would drive the attacking tribes away," suggested Brian.

"Mmm," said Maria, who was getting tired of history. "Let's stop being Bronze Age. I'm hungry."

They went down to the stream and ate their picnic with

Tom and Annie. Hairy swam to fetch the sticks they threw and tried to chase moorhens, but every time he barked at them he got a mouthful of water. He soon gave up and went over to the slope beneath Slug's parking place.

He spotted some holes in the side of the sandy bank and sniffed the scent of rabbits. He barked down the burrows, inviting them to come out and play, but not one appeared. Then he scrabbled away at the sandy slope with his forepaws, but still no rabbit accepted his noisy invitation.

Suddenly he gave an ear-splitting yowling bark and streaked down to the others by the stream. They all turned round in time to see the sandy, water-logged ground crumbling very slowly beneath Slug's back wheels. "OY!" shouted Tom warningly at Slug.

But Slug could do nothing. She was helpless as her back wheels began to sag, then sink, then drop backwards, as the ground gave way beneath her. Gently, very gently, her back went down, down, down, and her nose tipped further and further up towards the hilltop. Then she was almost upright, her headlights looking at the sky—then o-o-over she tipped: BOOINNG! She lay there, dazed, flat on her roof on the grass, her wheels spinning crazily.

"Rrrufff!" barked Hairy, dashing over to Slug and back again. "Rrrufff!"

"No, Hairy," said Maria. "Slug doesn't want her tummy tickled."

Tom set off to the nearest farm, and the others stood round poor little upside-down Slug and stared helplessly. When Tom came back with the farmer and his tractor, they roped Slug to the back of it. Then with a great deal of pushing and pulling they managed to get her standing on four wheels again. They finally pulled her up the slope on to the hard road.

"Phew!" said the farmer. "It was that sandy slope that did it: it was full of rabbit burrows. The heavy rain in the night must have soaked into it, and your dog started a small landslide. I'd better get this bit of field fenced off, then it won't happen again."

They all thanked him gratefully. Slug seemed all right. Her roof was bruised and dented, and she was a little shaky, but she started straight away and they began the drive home. However, just as they were approaching the town, she began to shiver and slow down. Tom drove into a lay-by and she stopped. Nothing Tom could do would persuade her to start again. She stood there, trembling, on her four small wheels.

"It's the shock," explained Annie. "She's had an awful experience. She's got delayed shock."

They all climbed out and stared helplessly at Slug once more. Even Hairy could only rub his nose sympathetically against her front bumper.

"Need some help?" asked a voice. A man in a blue boiler suit had strolled up.

"We're only about three miles from home," said Tom. "But we've got an invalid on our hands." He explained what had happened.

"No probs.," said the man. "Come on, we'll give her a piggy-back." He pointed in front of them, and there, further along the lay-by, stood a powerful car transporter —empty. "Get your shoulders behind her and we'll roll her on," said the driver. Tom took off Slug's handbrake, and she was soon up on the platform of the giant transporter. The two men fastened her tightly so she couldn't slip. "You'd better all have a lift in my cab," offered the driver. "Come on."

Brian and Maria followed their parents and managed the

high stretch up from one metal footrest to the next into the car transporter's cab. There was room for everyone; even Hairy had plenty of space between their feet and the front of the cab.

Maria was delighted. "It's just like a little room," she said. They stared at the two narrow bunk beds behind the driver.

"They're for when we're on long journeys, we can pull into a lay-by and have a kip," he explained.

"And there are even little curtains!" exclaimed Maria.

The seats were comfortable and very high up. "Wow," said Brian. "We'll be able to see everything for miles ahead."

"Let's go then," said the driver. With an enormous, vibrating roar, the huge transporter's engine started and they slowly pulled out of the lay-by.

Tom gave directions and they were soon pulling up in Mr Fortescue's petrol station forecourt. He came out and stared to see the way the Mablesdens *and* Slug had arrived.

They were sorry to say goodbye to the kind driver and even sorrier to leave Slug (who had easily rolled backwards off her piggy-back). Mr Fortescue was very sympathetic. "Now don't worry, all of you," he said. "I know she's due for her M.O.T. test, but I'll work on her all Sunday. I'll do my best for her. But don't forget — she's quite an old lady, really."

"Just what I said," nodded Tom, but he looked pretty depressed all the same.

"Perhaps we shouldn't have let her have that Last Fling, after all," said Annie. "She's had so much excitement today—perhaps it's been just too much for her system . . ."

It was a very long Sunday. Tom spent most of it pacing

up and down the garden. Brian and Maria moped about, and even Hairy didn't seem to notice whether the television was switched on or off. The phone rang at about eight o'clock in the evening. Tom snatched it up. Mr Fortescue spoke briefly.

"He says he's got her engine working OK," reported Tom, but he still looked worried. "The M.O.T. test is really stiff—and she *is* getting on a bit . . ."

Monday morning: no news. At lunchtime Tom was given a lift home by a friend: still no news. They all sat silent and glum, chewing their beefburgers as though they were made of cardboard.

"Bee-eeep! Bee-eeep! Bee-eeep!" A rattling chug came nearer down the street.

"I'd know that noise anywhere," cried Annie, dropping her knife and fork and rushing to the window.

"It's old Fortescue with Slug," cried Tom, his eyes shining. "She must have passed!" He raced out of the door and had his hand on Slug's bonnet before she'd come to a halt. Mr Fortescue climbed out grinning.

"A great old lady you've got there, Tom," he said. "They tried to find fault wth her brakes, lights, steering, gearbox, engine—they gave her a real going over, but afterwards they said there was no reason why she shouldn't manage another year on the road."

The family cheered and Hairy ran round and round Slug, wagging his tail joyfully. Slug herself thought it was all a lot of fuss about nothing. She'd been *quite* sure the M.O.T. test would show there was nothing really wrong with her.

But all the same, her radiator grille grinned a wide shining grin in the sunshine. Perhaps they'd treat her with a little more respect now she was a grand old lady. Especially that four-footed hairy idiot . . .

THE COUNTY SHOW

———•———

"Don't sit on that stool," yelled Tom, as Maria came into the living room. "It's not for sitting on!" Maria was metres away from her father's home-made stool, but he had just put the final touches to the woven seat and was determined that nothing should happen to it before the County Show.

Maria shrugged, and drifted into the kitchen where Annie was bending down to lift baking tins from the oven. Maria looked at the good things to eat cooling on the kitchen table. "Don't touch those custard tarts," warned her mother. "They're for the Show."

"They're a bit wobbly," said Maria tactlessly, peering at the tarts.

"Oh, really, Maria," snapped her mother. She knew the tarts were rather wobbly and this made her even crosser. "Have you nothing better to do than criticize other people's handiwork? Why don't you go and practise your handwriting? Then perhaps you could go in for the Handwriting Competition at the Show?"

Maria flounced off. "I've been told off twice, for nothing—it's not fair!" Her mother was mean to suggest the Handwriting Competition—everyone knew Maria's writing was awful. On Parents' Evenings, teacher after

teacher had said, "Her written work is interesting . . ."
But then they always added with a sigh: "If only Maria
could tidy up her handwriting a little . . ."

Maria personally thought it was the horrid wide-
nibbed cartridge pens her Auntie Clare gave her every
Christmas. But if she complained somebody always said
either: "You mustn't look a gift horse in the mouth," or
"A bad workman always blames his tools," so she was
still in the wrong. Maria sighed.

She mooched into Brian's room. "Don't touch that,"
he shouted, the moment she appeared in the doorway.
His newly varnished model of Concorde stood in the
centre of the table.

"I suppose you're entering that for the County Show?"
asked Maria, although she knew the answer already.
Brian nodded absent-mindedly, his tongue between his
teeth, and frowned at the entry form he was filling in.

Maria sighed heavily. She went and sat on her bed and
stared into space. The County Show was tomorrow.
Everyone else was dead keen and going in for
competitions and things. Why wasn't there something
she could do? It was going to be a rotten afternoon out if
they just trudged from the custard tarts to the stools to
the model aeroplanes—big deal.

At this moment Maria's bedroom door was flung wide
open and Hairy rushed in. He bounded up on to the bed
and walked all over her lap, nuzzling up to her
affectionately. "Hairy!" she yelled, as a thought occurred
to her.

Hairy jumped down and stood looking at her with his
head on one side—he hadn't meant to upset her. "You
clever dog," said Maria, ruffling him round the head and
ears, much to his delight. "You clever, *amazing* dog—

you came in *just* at the right moment. There'll be a Dog Show, of course, a *dog* show, Hairy. I'll enter you, you clever old thing. Who cares about soppy handwriting, anyway?"

That evening Tom took the stool, the model of Concorde and Annie's baking to the County Show ground. "I'll come and help you carry," said Maria.

"Oh, thanks," said her father, surprised at her last-minute show of interest.

The huge marquees were dotted all over the show ground. Other competitors were there, also carrying precious loads to arrange in the best way to catch the judges' eyes. Tom and Maria carefully avoided stumbling over tent ropes and pegs. "Here's the cookery section," said Tom. "And there's the furniture over there."

"I'll leave Concorde here," said Maria, "and just have a little look around. Back in ten minutes." Before Tom could ask questions, she was gone.

She went straight to the pets' tent. A gentleman with a label "Steward" was there, keeping an eye on cages of rabbits, pigeons, hens, mice and other small animals. "Good evening, Mr . . . er . . . Steward," said Maria nervously. "Will you be having a Dog Show?"

"There are several competitions for dogs and their owners," said the man, handing her an entry form. "Fifty pence to enter each one. Turn up here tomorrow at three o'clock. With your dog, of course. Money in advance."

Maria had thought to bring the pound she had saved to spend at the Show. That meant Hairy could enter for two competitions. She glanced at the list.

1 MOST OBEDIENT DOG. Mmm, Hairy was too inclined to go his own way for that.

2 BEST GROOMED DOG. Definitely not!

3 BIGGEST DOG. He *was* pretty big.

4 HAIRIEST DOG—oh, surely no other dog could be hairier than Hairy!

5 SMALLEST DOG. No; even when he was little he was big, thought Maria.

6 MOST INTELLIGENT DOG. Well, *they* all thought he was amazingly intelligent—but would the judges?

She handed over the pound and the form she'd filled in. "Hairy and intelligent, is he?" smiled the man. "See you tomorrow then." She hurried back to where Tom was waiting for her.

"Had a good look round?" he asked.

"Oh, yes," she nodded vaguely. She didn't want to tell anyone—yet.

Next day the Mablesdens arrived at the show ground in good time. They parked Slug in the car park between a horse box and a rather smelly farm trailer. Slug was relieved that Tom shut her ventilator flaps before they left her; she was *very* sensitive to her surroundings.

Maria had Hairy on a lead. "I don't know why you've brought him," said Brian.

"You know he gets lonely on his own at home," said Maria. "Besides, I wanted company."

"You've got us," said Brian.

"You'll be too busy looking at models and things," said Maria. She still hadn't told anyone about entering Hairy for the competitions. They all arranged to meet by the ambulance tent at four o'clock, then went their own ways.

Maria and Hairy found plenty to look at and it was very soon five to three.

"Come on, Hairy, your big moment."

They found the marquee where the Dog Competitions were going to take place. Maria looked round as the first three competitions took place. There were some tiny toy dogs and some huge Boxers and even a Great Dane. It was a good thing Maria hadn't entered Hairy for the Biggest Dog Competition—he wouldn't have stood a chance. When the Hairiest Dog Competition began, she was number 17. She stood in a line with other owners, Hairy pressed to her legs. Her heart was thumping with nervousness—and then with disappointment: there were some dogs which were *very* much hairier then Hairy. A couple of Old English Sheepdogs and Afghan Hounds had amazingly long fur, far longer than his. Hairy just looked so hairy because he'd always been running about or pushing through hedges or rolling in the thistles. Maria looked along the line. Yes, an Afghan hound had won first prize.

She scuffed her sandal in the grass floor of the marquee, while Hairy looked up at her hopefully. She watched the fifth competition despondently, and then realized that it was ten minutes to four. They'd have to be going. She pulled Hairy towards the exit.

"Now for the last competition of the afternoon," announced her friend, Mr Steward: "'The Most Intelligent Dog.'"

Maria had forgotten the last competition. "They probably won't think he's intelligent at all," she thought sadly. She looked down at Hairy as he sat with his head on one side, watching the other dogs. He *did* look rather bedraggled, she had to admit. And perhaps even a bit . . . dim . . . to those who didn't know him.

"Six owners have entered their pets for this competition, and we want *them* to prove to the judges how intelligently their dogs respond to them—in any way they like," announced Mr Steward. "We'll start with Peke-a-Boo."

This was a tiny Pekinese dog whose lady owner looked rather bewildered at the task she'd been set. "Heel! Sit! Stay!" The little Peke obeyed perfectly with a charming toss of the head, then pawed at her lady owner's handbag for a sugar-lump reward. She was given it, to applause from the onlookers.

Next followed Bob, an English Sheepdog, then an Alsatian, a Labrador and a bright little Cocker Spaniel called Curly. They all did exactly as their owners told them and sat wagging their tails waiting for the next command. Curly earned a special cheer by 'singing' God Save the Queen with her owner.

"Ridiculous what they get us to do, isn't it?" grunted the Labrador at Hairy's side. Hairy agreed. He hoped Maria would give him some sensible tasks.

"Oh, Hairy," whispered Maria. "Why on earth did I enter you for this?" She was trembling with nerves. Hairy turned and licked her hand encouragingly.

Mr Steward spoke again, "Now it's time for our final contestant: Hairy Mablesden!" There was a slight murmur at his unusual name, then everyone was quiet.

Maria had to go into the centre of the ring. She cleared her throat.

"Do you like jelly, Hairy?" she asked. Hairy sat silent. "Do you like cabbage, Hairy?" Hairy just sat and looked into the distance. "Custard?" asked Maria. Hairy yawned. "A plate of raw liver?" asked Maria. Hairy leapt up and barked enthusiastically.

Maria smiled with relief as the audience laughed. She knew that Hairy wasn't very good at sitting and staying and heeling—he was always too bouncy and eager. So now she was going to try something quite different: he knew most about what he saw on television, so she was going to show everyone that.

"How many Beatles are there?" she asked clearly. Hairy knew the answer to that: he gave four loud barks in reply. Everyone clapped. "How many people travel in the Batmobile?" asked Maria. Hairy gave two hearty barks for Batman and Robin. He was a great fan of theirs.

"Do you like Catwoman?" asked Maria. Hairy *hated* Catwoman. He snarled menacingly. The audience clapped and cheered. "What an *amazing* dog!" said someone near Maria. She began to enjoy herself.

"Now tell everyone your favourite programme," she said. She started to whistle. Everyone listened attentively. Even the other dogs looked interested. First she whistled 'Baa baa, black sheep'. Hairy just looked at her.

Then she whistled 'Oranges and lemons'. Hairy went on listening quietly. Next she whistled a sailor's hornpipe. Hairy leapt to his feet and barked happily: it was the signature tune of 'Blue Peter,' the programme which starred lots of dogs. Hairy loved it.

Everyone clapped again. "He's remarkable," said a lady in a large hat.

Maria felt much braver. She was really enjoying showing Hairy off. Everyone in the marquee was listening. "Last of all," she said, "what do you think of *this* programme?" She started to whistle the first few distinctive bars of the 'Dr Who' signature tune. Hairy was always scared by the monsters in this programme and usually watched it from behind Tom's chair. He put up his head and howled dismally. The he slumped down into a

ball and put his paws over his ears, still howling miserably. Everyone cheered and laughed.

"Tremendous," they shouted.

"He's won!" The chief judge stood up, still laughing himself. "Yes, by unanimous decision of the judges, the prize for the most intelligent dog goes to Hairy Mablesden."

"Fantastic," said Tom and Annie to one another. They had just come in at the back of the marquee to see what the cheering and laughing was about. Brian too, had ducked under the side of the canvas and couldn't believe his eyes as he saw Maria shyly walking with Hairy to the judge's table.

"For the owner of the brightest dog there's a very nice pen," said the judge. "And for the dog himself, there's a fine new leather collar, inscribed with the date and the occasion." He handed them over with a beaming smile. "Well done, both of you. You deserve one another."

Maria blushed and patted Hairy to hide her red cheeks. The family pounced upon them and led them triumphantly to the car park.

"Well done," said Tom. "My stool collapsed."

"My custard tart was runny," said Annie.

"Concorde's paint came off all over the judges' hands," grinned Brian.

"But you and Hairy saved our honour," said Annie. "Clever dog!" she said, slapping his sides affectionately.

They got into Slug and joined the slowly moving line of cars leaving the Show. All the family was talking at once. Slug gradually learned what had happened as she chugged along.

"It's not possible . . ." she rumbled to herself. She wove to and fro in the queue of cars, shaking her bonnet in disbelief. "It's just not possible. That hairy idiot is the Most Intelligent Dog in the Show? Then I'm the Batmobile!"

"Rrruff, rrruff, rrruff!" chortled Hairy, watching her speedometer creep up to eight miles an hour. "*That'll* be the day!"

The Railway Cat and Digby
PHYLLIS ARKLE

Further adventures of Alfie the railway cat, who always seems to be in Leading Railman Hack's bad books. Alfie is a smart cat, a lot smarter than many people think, and he would like to be friends with Hack. But when he tries to improve matters by 'helping' Hack's dog, Digby, win a prize at the local show, the situation rapidly goes from bad to worse!

Burglar Bells
JOHN ESCOTT

In horror, Bernie and Lee watch a man climbing through the window of an empty house. Is he a burglar? When news breaks out of a burglary in that road, the pair are convinced it was the man they saw – who is going to marry Miss Daisy, the charming school secretary. What should they do? Find out in this exciting, fast-moving adventure.

Mr Berry's Ice-Cream Parlour
JENNIFER ZABEL

Carl is thrilled when Mr Berry, the new lodger, comes to stay. But when Mr Berry announces his plan to open an ice-cream parlour, Carl can hardly believe it. And this is just the start of the excitements in store when Mr Berry walks through the door.

The Conker as Hard as a Diamond
CHRIS POWLING
Last conker season, Little Alpesh had lost every single game, but this year he's determined it will be different. This year he's going to win, and he won't stop until he's Conker Champion of the Universe! The trouble is, only a conker as hard as a diamond will make it possible – and where on earth is he going to find one?

Pugwash and the Mutiny and Pugwash and the Fancy-Dress Party
JOHN RYAN
Two hilarious stories starring that most amiable of pirates, Captain Pugwash. When he and his cabin boy Tom are cast ashore, things don't work out quite as the mutinous crew had planned, for the dastardly Cut-throat Jake and his bloodthirsty band make an unexpected entrance. And that same evil villain is out to spoil Pugwash's devious plan for a fancy-dress ball – which would have filled the treasure-chest with gleaming gold, silver and jewels!

The Dead Letter Box
JAN MARK
Louie got the idea from an old film which showed how spies left their letters in a secret place – a dead letter box. It was just the kind of thing that she and Glenda needed to help them keep in touch. And she knew the perfect place for it!

Duck Boy
CHRISTOBEL MATTINGLEY
The holiday at Mrs Perry's farm doesn't start very well for Adam. His older brother and sister don't want to spend any time with him; they say he's too young. At first he's bored and lonely, but then he discovers the creek and meets two old ducks who obviously need help. Every year their eggs are stolen by rats or foxes, so Adam strikes a bargain with them: he'll help guard their nest, if they'll let him learn to swim in their creek.

Three Cheers for Ragdolly Anna
JEAN KENWARD
Being a very special kind of doll, Ragdolly Anna is trusted to do all sorts of things for the Little Dressmaker – but somehow nothing ever seems to go right. Her balcony garden turns into a jungle, a misguided stranger hands her into a lost property office, and she's nearly bought as a fairy for a Christmas tree!

Return to Oz
ALISTAIR HEDLEY
Dorothy knows that her friends and the Emerald City must be saved from the evil Nome King, the cruel Princess Mombi and the terrifying squealing Wheelers. So, with some strange companions, Tik-Tok, Jack Pumpkinhead and a talking hen, Billina, she sets off on a frightening, mysterious and exciting adventure.

Tales from The Wind in the Willows
KENNETH GRAHAME
'Isn't it a bit dull at times?' Mole asked Ratty. 'Just you and the river, and no one else to pass a word with?'

Mole couldn't have been more wrong about life along the riverbank. There were all sorts of animals living in and by the river, and one in particular who was anything *but* dull – Mr Toad! A delightfully new edition, enchantingly illustrated by Margaret Gordon, and especially abridged for younger readers to enjoy.

Eloise
KAY THOMPSON
Eloise is six. She lives at the Plaza Hotel (where her mother knows The Owner) with her dog, her turtle and her English Nanny. If there's one thing Eloise never is, it's bored. She never has a spare moment because there's just so much to do. There's the Lobby to check out, Skipperdee's ears to plait, waiters and switchboard operators to help, French lessons to ignore and, above all, other guests to investigate. Eloise is wildly funny, wickedly inventive and totally unpredictable.

Cup Final for Charlie
JOY ALLEN
Uncle Tom turns up with a spare ticket for the Cup Final at Wembley. But will Charlie be allowed to go? In the second story, Charlie is given a brand-new pair of shiny red boots, which turn out to be far more useful than anyone could have imagined.

Victor the Vulture
JANE HOLIDAY

Everyone in his class had a pet except Garth, so when his father won a vulture in a raffle it seemed like the answer to his prayers. But the local council have rules about their tenants keeping pets.

Professor Branestawm's Mouse War and Professor Branestawm's Building Bust-Up
NORMAN HUNTER

Two more peculiar inventions by the hilarious Professor. The first story features a cat-shaped balloon to rid Great Pagwell of its mice problem, and the other tells of a house-building machine.

Katy and the Nurgla
HARRY SECOMBE

Katy had the whole beach to herself, until an old tired monster swam up to the very rocks where she was sitting reading. Harry Secombe's first book for children has all the best ingredients in the right proportions: a monster, a spaceship, adventure, humour and more than a touch of happy sadness.

The Ghost at No. 13
GYLES BRANDRETH

Hamlet Brown's sister, Susan, is just too perfect. Everything she does is praised and Hamlet is in despair – until a ghost comes to stay for a holiday and helps him to find an exciting idea for his school project!

Radio Detective
JOHN ESCOTT

A piece of amazing deduction by the Roundbay Radio Detective when Donald, the radio's young presenter, solves a mystery but finds out more than anyone expects.

Chris and the Dragon
FAY SAMPSON

Chris always seems to be in trouble but he does try extra hard to be good when he is chosen to play Joseph in the school nativity play. This hilarious story ends with a glorious celebration of the Chinese New Year.